TIGGER TALES

by A. A. MILNE

illustrations by ERNEST H. SHEPARD

Dutton Children's Books

NEW YORK

Library of Congress Cataloging-in-Publication Data
Milne, A.A. (Alan Alexander), 1882-1956
[House at Pooh Corner. Selections]
Tigger tales/by A. A. Milne; illustrations by Ernest H. Shepard.
p. cm.
"All selections from The House at Pooh Corner"—T.p. verso.
Contents: Tigger comes to the forest and has breakfast—It is shown that tiggers don't climb trees—Tigger is unbounced.
Summary: A collection of three tales about the bouncing Tigger and his adventures in the Hundred-Acre Wood..
ISBN 0-525-46941-9
[1. Tigers—Fiction. 2. Toys—Fiction.] I. Shepard, Ernest H. (Ernest Howard), 1879-1976. II. Title..
PZ7.M64 Tk 2002   [Fic]—dc21   2001047337

Published in the United States by Dutton Children's Books,
a division of Penguin Putnam Books for Young Readers
345 Hudson Street, New York, New York 10014
www.penguinputnam.com
Designed by Daniel Hosek
First Edition
Printed in China
1 3 5 7 9 10 8 6 4 2

CONTENTS

Tigger Comes to the Forest
and Has Breakfast

1

It Is Shown That Tiggers
Don't Climb Trees

13

Tigger Is Unbounced

27

Tigger Comes to the Forest and Has Breakfast

Winnie-the-Pooh woke up suddenly in the middle of the night and listened. Then he got out of bed, and lit his candle, and stumped across the room to see if anybody was trying to get into his honey-cupboard, and they weren't, so he stumped back again, blew out his candle, and got into bed. Then he heard the noise again.

"Is that you, Piglet?" he said.

But it wasn't.

"Come in, Christopher Robin," he said.

But Christopher Robin didn't.

"Tell me about it tomorrow, Eeyore," said Pooh sleepily.

But the noise went on.

"*Worraworraworraworraworra,*" said Whatever-it-was, and Pooh found that he wasn't asleep after all.

"What can it be?" he thought. "There are lots of noises in the Forest, but this is a different one. It isn't a growl, and it isn't a purr, and it isn't a bark, and it isn't the noise-you-make-before-beginning-a-piece-of-poetry, but it's a noise of some kind, made by a strange animal. And he's making it outside my door. So I shall get up and ask him not to do it."

He got out of bed and opened his front door.

"Hallo!" said Pooh, in case there was anything outside.

"Hallo!" said Whatever-it-was.

"Oh!" said Pooh. "Hallo!"

"Hallo!"

"Oh, *there* you are!" said Pooh. "Hallo!"

"Hallo!" said the Strange Animal, wondering how long this was going on.

Pooh was just going to say "Hallo!" for the fourth time when he thought that he wouldn't so he said: "Who is it?" instead.

"Me," said a voice.

"Oh!" said Pooh. "Well, come here."

So Whatever-it-was came here, and in the light of the candle he and Pooh looked at each other.

"I'm Pooh," said Pooh.

"I'm Tigger," said Tigger.

"Oh!" said Pooh, for he had never seen an animal like this before. "Does Christopher Robin know about you?"

"Of course he does," said Tigger.

"Well," said Pooh, "it's the middle of the night, which is a good time for going to sleep. And tomorrow morning we'll have some honey for breakfast. Do Tiggers like honey?"

"They like everything," said Tigger cheerfully.

"Then if they like going to sleep on the floor, I'll go back to bed," said Pooh, "and we'll do things in the morning. Good night." And he got back into bed and went fast asleep.

When he awoke in the morning, the first thing he saw was Tigger, sitting in front of the glass and looking at himself.

"Hallo!" said Pooh.

"Hallo!" said Tigger. "I've found somebody just like me. I thought I was the only one of them."

Pooh got out of bed, and began to explain what a looking-glass was, but just as he was getting to the interesting part, Tigger said:

"Excuse me a moment, but there's something climbing up your table," and with one loud *Worraworraworraworraworra* he jumped at the end of the tablecloth, pulled it to the ground, wrapped himself up in it three times, rolled to the other end of the room, and, after a terrible struggle, got his head into the daylight again, and said cheerfully: "Have I won?"

"That's my tablecloth," said Pooh, as he began to unwind Tigger.

"I wondered what it was," said Tigger.

"It goes on the table and you put things on it."

"Then why did it try to bite me when I wasn't looking?"

"I don't *think* it did," said Pooh.

"It tried," said Tigger, "but I was too quick for it."

Pooh put the tablecloth back on the table, and he put a large honey-pot on the cloth, and they sat down to breakfast. As soon as they sat down, Tigger took a large mouthful of honey… and he looked up at the ceiling with his head on one side, and made exploring noises with his tongue and considering noises, and what-have-we-got-*here* noises…and then he said in a very decided voice:

"Tiggers don't like honey."

"Oh!" said Pooh, and tried to make it sound Sad and Regretful. "I thought they liked everything."

"Everything except honey," said Tigger.

Pooh felt rather pleased about this, and said that, as soon as he had finished his own breakfast, he would take Tigger round to see Piglet's house, and Tigger could try some of Piglet's haycorns.

"Thank you, Pooh," said Tigger, "because haycorns is really what Tiggers like best."

So after breakfast they went round to see Piglet, and Pooh explained as they went that Piglet was a Very Small Animal who didn't like bouncing, and asked Tigger not to be too Bouncy just at first. And Tigger, who had been hiding behind trees and jumping out on Pooh's shadow when it wasn't looking, said that Tiggers were only bouncy before breakfast, and that as soon as they had had a few haycorns they became Quiet and Refined. So by and by they knocked at the door of Piglet's house.

"Hallo, Pooh," said Piglet.

"Hallo, Piglet. This is Tigger."

"Oh, is it?" said Piglet, and he edged round to the other side of the table. "I thought Tiggers were smaller than that."

"Not the big ones," said Tigger.

"They like haycorns," said Pooh, "so that's what we've come for, because poor Tigger hasn't had any breakfast yet."

Piglet pushed the bowl of haycorns towards Tigger, and said: "Help yourself," and then he got close up to Pooh and felt much braver, and said, "So you're Tigger? Well, well!" in a careless sort of voice. But Tigger said nothing because his mouth was full of haycorns….

After a long munching noise he said:

"Ee-ers o i a-ors."

And when Pooh and Piglet said "What?" he said "Skoos ee," and went outside for a moment.

When he came back he said firmly:

"Tiggers don't like haycorns."

"But you said they liked everything except honey," said Pooh.

"Everything except honey and haycorns," explained Tigger.

When he heard this Pooh said, "Oh, I see!" and Piglet, who was rather glad that Tiggers didn't like haycorns, said, "What about thistles?"

"Thistles," said Tigger, "is what Tiggers like best."

"Then let's go along and see Eeyore," said Piglet.

So the three of them went; and after they had walked and walked and walked, they came to the part of the Forest where Eeyore was.

"Hallo, Eeyore!" said Pooh. "This is Tigger."

"What is?" said Eeyore.

"This," explained Pooh and Piglet together, and Tigger smiled his happiest smile and said nothing.

Eeyore walked all round Tigger one way, and then turned and walked all round him the other way.

"What did you say it was?" he asked.

"Tigger."

"Ah!" said Eeyore.

"He's just come," explained Piglet.

"Ah!" said Eeyore again.

He thought for a long time and then said: "When is he going?"

Pooh explained to Eeyore that Tigger was a great friend of Christopher Robin's, who had come to stay in the Forest, and Piglet explained to Tigger that he mustn't mind what Eeyore said because he was always gloomy; and Eeyore explained to Piglet that, on the contrary, he was feeling particularly cheerful this morning; and Tigger explained to anybody who was listening that he hadn't had any breakfast yet.

"I knew there was something," said Pooh. "Tiggers always eat thistles, so that was why we came to see you, Eeyore."

"Don't mention it, Pooh."

"Oh, Eeyore, I didn't mean that I didn't *want* to see you—"

"Quite—quite. But your new stripy friend—naturally, he wants his breakfast. What did you say his name was?"

"Tigger."

"Then come this way, Tigger."

Eeyore led the way to the most thistly-looking patch of thistles that ever was, and waved a hoof at it.

"A little patch I was keeping for my birthday," he said; "but, after all, what are birthdays? Here today and gone tomorrow. Help yourself, Tigger."

Tigger thanked him and looked a little anxiously at Pooh.

"Are these really thistles?" he whispered.

"Yes," said Pooh.

"What Tiggers like best?"

"That's right," said Pooh.

"I see," said Tigger.

So he took a large mouthful, and he gave a large crunch.

"*Ow!*" said Tigger.

He sat down and put his paw in his mouth.

"What's the matter?" asked Pooh.

"*Hot!*" mumbled Tigger.

"Your friend," said Eeyore, "appears to have bitten on a bee."

Pooh's friend stopped shaking his head to get the prickles out, and explained that Tiggers didn't like thistles.

"Then why bend a perfectly good one?" asked Eeyore.

"But you said," began Pooh—"you *said* that Tiggers like everything except honey and haycorns."

"*And* thistles," said Tigger, who was now running around in circles with his tongue hanging out.

Pooh looked at him sadly.

"What are we going to do?" he asked Piglet.

Piglet knew the answer to that, and he said at once that they must go and see Christopher Robin.

"You'll find him with Kanga," said Eeyore. He came close to Pooh, and said in a loud whisper:

"*Could* you ask your friend to do his exercises somewhere else? I shall be having lunch directly, and don't want it bounced on just before I begin. A trifling matter, and fussy of me, but we all have our little ways."

Pooh nodded solemnly and called to Tigger.

"Come along and we'll go and see Kanga. She's sure to have lots of breakfast for you."

Tigger finished his last circle and came up to Pooh and Piglet.

"Hot!" he explained with a large and friendly smile. "Come on!" and he rushed off.

Pooh and Piglet walked slowly after him. And as they walked Piglet said nothing, because he couldn't think of anything, and Pooh said nothing, because he was thinking of a poem. And when he thought of it he began:

> *What shall we do about*
> *   poor little Tigger?*
> *If he never eats nothing he'll*
> *   never get bigger.*
> *He doesn't like honey and haycorns*
> *   and thistles*
> *Because of the taste and because of*
> *   the bristles.*
> *And all the good things which an*
> *   animal likes*
> *Have the wrong sort of swallow or*
> *   too many spikes.*

"He's quite big enough anyhow," said Piglet.

"He isn't *really* very big."

"Well, he *seems* so."

Pooh was thoughtful when he heard this, and then he murmured to himself:

> *But whatever his weight in pounds,*
> *   shillings, and ounces,*
> *He always seems bigger*
> *   because of his bounces.*

"And that's the whole poem," he said. "Do you like it, Piglet?"

"All except the shillings," said Piglet. "I don't think they ought to be there."

"They wanted to come in after the pounds," explained Pooh, "so I let them. It is the best way to write poetry, letting things come."

"Oh, I didn't know," said Piglet.

Tigger had been bouncing in front of them all this time, turning round every now and then to ask, "Is this the way?"—and now at last they came in sight of Kanga's house, and there was Christopher Robin. Tigger rushed up to him.

"Oh, there you are, Tigger!" said Christopher Robin. "I knew you'd be somewhere."

"I've been finding things in the Forest," said Tigger importantly. "I've found a pooh and a piglet and an eeyore, but I can't find any breakfast."

Pooh and Piglet came up and hugged Christopher Robin, and explained what had been happening.

"Don't *you* know what Tiggers like?" asked Pooh.

"I expect if I thought very hard I should," said Christopher Robin, "but I *thought* Tigger knew."

"I do," said Tigger. "Everything there is in the world except honey and haycorns and—what were those hot things called?"

"Thistles."

"Yes, and those."

"Oh, well then, Kanga can give you some breakfast."

So they went into Kanga's house, and when Roo had said, "Hallo, Pooh" and "Hallo, Piglet" once, and "Hallo, Tigger" twice, because he had never said it before and it sounded funny, they told Kanga what they wanted, and Kanga said very kindly, "Well, look in my cupboard, Tigger dear, and see what you'd like." Because she knew at once that, however big Tigger seemed to be, he wanted as much kindness as Roo.

"Shall I look, too?" said Pooh, who was beginning to feel a little eleven o'clockish. And he found a small tin of condensed milk, and something seemed to tell him that Tiggers didn't like this, so he took it into a corner by itself, and went with it to see that nobody interrupted it.

But the more Tigger put his nose into this and his paw into that, the more things he found which Tiggers didn't like. And when he had found everything in the cupboard, and couldn't eat any of it, he said to Kanga, "What happens now?"

But Kanga and Christopher Robin and Piglet were all standing round Roo, watching him have his Extract of Malt. And Roo was saying "Must

I?" and Kanga was saying "Now, Roo dear, you remember what you promised."

"What is it?" whispered Tigger to Piglet.

"His Strengthening Medicine," said Piglet. "He hates it."

So Tigger came closer, and leant over the back of Roo's chair, and suddenly he put out his tongue, and took one large golollop, and, with a sudden jump of surprise, Kanga said, "Oh!" and then clutched at the spoon again just as it was disappearing, and pulled it safely back out of Tigger's mouth. But the Extract of Malt had gone.

"Tigger *dear*!" said Kanga.

"He's taken my medicine, he's taken my medicine, he's taken my medicine!" sang Roo happily, thinking it was a tremendous joke.

Then Tigger looked up at the ceiling, and closed his eyes, and his tongue went round and round his chops, in case he had left any outside, and a peaceful smile came over his face as he said, "So *that's* what Tiggers like!"

Which explains why he always lived at Kanga's house afterwards, and had Extract of Malt for breakfast, dinner, and tea. And sometimes, when Kanga thought he wanted strengthening, he had a spoonful or two of Roo's breakfast after meals as medicine.

"But *I* think," said Piglet to Pooh, "that he's been strengthened quite enough."

It Is Shown That Tiggers Don't Climb Trees

One day when Pooh was thinking, he thought he would go and see Eeyore, because he hadn't seen him since yesterday. And as he walked through the heather, singing to himself, he suddenly remembered that he hadn't seen Owl since the day before yesterday, so he thought that he would just look in at the Hundred Acre Wood on the way and see if Owl was at home.

Well, he went on singing, until he came to the part of the stream where the stepping-stones were, and when he was in the middle of the third stone, he began to wonder how Kanga and Roo and Tigger were getting on, because they all lived together in a different part of the Forest. And he thought, "I haven't seen Roo for a long time, and if I don't see him today it will be a still longer time." So he sat down on the stone in the middle of the stream and sang another verse of his song, while he wondered what to do.

The other verse of the song was like this:

I could spend a happy morning
Seeing Roo,
I could spend a happy morning
Being Pooh.
For it doesn't seem to matter,
If I don't get any fatter
(And I don't get any fatter),
What I do.

The sun was so delightfully warm, and the stone, which had been sitting in it for a long time, was so warm, too, that Pooh had almost decided to go on being Pooh in the middle of the stream for the rest of the morning, when he remembered Rabbit.

"Rabbit," said Pooh to himself. "I *like* talking to Rabbit. He talks about sensible things. He doesn't use long, difficult words, like Owl. He uses short, easy words, like 'What about lunch?' and 'Help yourself, Pooh.' I suppose *really,* I ought to go and see Rabbit."

Which made him think of another verse:

Oh, I like his way of talking,
Yes, I do.
It's the nicest way of talking
Just for two.
And a Help-yourself with Rabbit
Though it may become a habit,
Is a pleasant sort of habit
For a Pooh.

So when he had sung this, he got up off his stone, walked back across the stream, and set off for Rabbit's house.

But he hadn't got far before he began to say to himself:

"Yes, but suppose Rabbit is out?"

"Or suppose I get stuck in his front door again, coming out, as I did once when his front door wasn't big enough?"

"Because I *know* I'm not getting fatter, but his front door may be getting thinner."

"So wouldn't it be better if—"

And all the time he was saying things like this he was going more and more westerly, without thinking…until suddenly he found himself at his own front door again.

And it was eleven o'clock.

Which was Time-for-a-little-something....

Half an hour later he was doing what he had always really meant to do, he was stumping off to Piglet's house. And as he walked, he wiped his mouth with the back of his paw, and sang rather a fluffy song through the fur. It went like this:

> *I could spend a happy morning*
> *Seeing Piglet.*
> *And I couldn't spend a happy morning*
> *Not seeing Piglet.*
> *And it doesn't seem to matter*
> *If I don't see Owl and Eeyore*
> *(or any of the others),*
> *And I'm not going to see Owl or Eeyore*
> *(or any of the others)*
> *Or Christopher Robin.*

Written down, like this, it doesn't seem a very good song, but coming through pale fawn fluff at about half-past eleven on a very sunny morning, it seemed to Pooh to be one of the best songs he had ever sung. So he went on singing it.

Piglet was busy digging a small hole in the ground outside his house.

"Hallo, Piglet," said Pooh.

"Hallo, Pooh," said Piglet, giving a jump of surprise. "I knew it was you."

"So did I," said Pooh. "What are you doing?"

"I'm planting a haycorn, Pooh, so that it can grow up into an oak-tree, and have lots of haycorns just outside the front door instead of having to walk miles and miles, do you see, Pooh?"

"Supposing it doesn't?" said Pooh.

"It will, because Christopher Robin says it will, so that's why I'm planting it."

"Well," said Pooh, "if I plant a honeycomb outside my house, then it will grow up into a beehive."

Piglet wasn't quite sure about this.

"Or a *piece* of a honeycomb," said Pooh, "so as not to waste too much. Only then I might only get a piece of a beehive, and it might be the wrong piece, where the bees were buzzing and not hunnying. Bother."

Piglet agreed that that would be rather bothering.

"Besides, Pooh, it's a very difficult thing, planting unless you know how to do it," he said; and he put the acorn in the hole he had made, and covered it up with earth, and jumped on it.

"I do know," said Pooh, "because Christopher Robin gave me a mastershalum seed, and I planted it, and I'm going to have mastershalums all over the front door."

"I thought they were called nasturtiums," said Piglet timidly, as he went on jumping.

"No," said Pooh. "Not these. These are called mastershalums."

When Piglet had finished jumping, he wiped his paws on his front, and said, "What shall we do now?" and Pooh said, "Let's go and see Kanga and Roo and Tigger," and Piglet said, "Y-yes. L-let's"—because he was still a little anxious about Tigger, who was a Very Bouncy Animal, with a way of saying How-do-you-do,

which always left your ears full of sand, even after Kanga had said, "Gently, Tigger dear," and had helped you up again. So they set off for Kanga's house.

Now it happened that Kanga had felt rather motherly that morning, and Wanting to Count Things—like Roo's vests, and how many pieces of soap there were left, and the two clean spots in Tigger's feeder; so she had sent them out with a packet of watercress sandwiches for Roo and a packet of extract-of-malt sandwiches for Tigger, to have a nice long morning in the Forest not getting into mischief. And off they had gone.

And as they went, Tigger told Roo (who wanted to know) all about the things that Tiggers could do.

"Can they fly?" asked Roo.

"Yes," said Tigger, "they're very good flyers, Tiggers are. Stornry good flyers."

"Oo!" said Roo. "Can they fly as well as Owl?"

"Yes," said Tigger. "Only they don't want to."

"Why don't they want to?"

"Well, they just don't like it, somehow."

Roo couldn't understand this, because he thought it would be lovely to be able to fly, but Tigger said it was difficult to explain to anybody who wasn't a Tigger himself.

"Well," said Roo, "can they jump as far as Kangas?"

"Yes," said Tigger. "When they want to."

"I *love* jumping," said Roo. "Let's see who can jump farthest, you or me."

"*I* can," said Tigger. "But we mustn't stop now, or we shall be late."

"Late for what?"

"For whatever we want to be in time for," said Tigger, hurrying on.

In a little while they came to the Six Pine Trees.

"I can swim," said Roo. "I fell into the river, and I swimmed. Can Tiggers swim?"

"Of course they can. Tiggers can do everything."

"Can they climb trees better than Pooh?" asked Roo, stopping under the tallest Pine Tree, and looking up at it.

"Climbing trees is what they do best," said Tigger. "Much better than Poohs."

"Could they climb this one?"

"They're always climbing trees like that," said Tigger. "Up and down all day."

"Oo, Tigger, are they *really*?"

"I'll show you," said Tigger bravely, "and you can sit on my back and watch me." For of all the things which he had said Tiggers could do, the only one he felt really certain about was climbing trees.

"Oo, Tigger, oo, Tigger, oo, Tigger!" squeaked Roo excitedly.

So he sat on Tigger's back and up they went.

And for the first ten feet Tigger said happily to himself, "Up we go!"

And for the next ten feet he said:

"I always *said* that Tiggers could climb trees."

And for the next ten feet he said:

"Not that it's easy, mind you."

And for the next ten feet he said:

"Of course, there's the coming-down too. Backwards."

And then he said:

"Which will be difficult..."

"Unless one fell..."

"When it would be..."

"EASY."

And at the word "easy" the branch he was standing on broke suddenly, and he just managed to clutch at the one above him as he felt himself going...and then slowly he got his chin over it...and then one back paw...and then the other...until at last he was sitting on it, breathing very quickly, and wishing that he had gone in for swimming instead.

Roo climbed off, and sat down next to him.

"Oo, Tigger," he said excitedly, "are we at the top?"

"No," said Tigger.

"Are we going to the top?"

"No," said Tigger.

"Oh," said Roo rather sadly. And then he went on hopefully: "That was a lovely bit just now, when you pretended we were going to fall-bump-to-the-bottom, and we didn't. Will you do that bit again?"

"NO," said Tigger.

Roo was silent for a little while, and then he said, "Shall we eat our sandwiches, Tigger?" And Tigger said, "Yes, where are they?" And Roo said, "At the bottom of the tree." And Tigger said, "I don't think we'd better eat them just yet." So they didn't.

By and by Pooh and Piglet came along. Pooh was telling Piglet in a singing voice that it didn't seem to matter, if he didn't get any fatter, and he didn't *think* he was getting any fatter, what he did; and Piglet was wondering how long it would be before his haycorn came up.

"Look, Pooh!" said Piglet suddenly. "There's something in one of the Pine Trees."

"So there is!" said Pooh, looking up wonderingly. "There's an Animal."

Piglet took Pooh's arm, in case Pooh was frightened.

"Is it One of the Fiercer Animals?" he said, looking the other way.

Pooh nodded.

"It's a Jagular," he said.

"What do Jagulars do?" asked Piglet, hoping that they wouldn't.

"They hide in the branches of trees, and drop on you as you go underneath," said Pooh. "Christopher Robin told me."

"Perhaps we better hadn't go underneath, Pooh. In case he dropped and hurt himself."

"They don't hurt themselves," said Pooh. "They're such very good droppers."

Piglet still felt that to be underneath a Very Good Dropper would be a Mistake, and he was just going to hurry back for something which he had forgotten when the Jagular called out to them.

"Help! Help!" it called.

"That's what Jagulars always do," said Pooh, much interested. "They call 'Help! Help!' and then when you look up, they drop on you."

"I'm looking *down,*" cried Piglet loudly, so as the Jagular shouldn't do the wrong thing by accident.

Something very excited next to the Jagular heard him, and squeaked:

"Pooh and Piglet! Pooh and Piglet!"

All of a sudden Piglet felt that it was a much nicer day than he had thought it was. All warm and sunny—

"Pooh!" he cried. "I believe it's Tigger and Roo!"

"So it is," said Pooh. "I thought it was a Jagular and another Jagular."

"Hallo, Roo!" called Piglet. "What are you doing?"

"We can't get down, we can't get down!" cried Roo. "Isn't it fun? Pooh, isn't it fun, Tigger and I are living in a tree, like Owl, and we're going to stay here for ever and ever. I can see Piglet's house from here. Aren't we high? Is Owl's house as high up as this?"

"How did you get there, Roo?" asked Piglet.

"On Tigger's back! And Tiggers can't climb downwards, because their tails get in the way, only upwards, and Tigger forgot about that when we started, and he's only just remembered. So we've got to stay here for ever and ever—unless we go higher. What did you say, Tigger? Oh, Tigger says if we go higher we shan't be able to see Piglet's house so well, so we're going to stop here."

"Piglet," said Pooh solemnly, when he had heard all this, "what shall we do?" And he began to eat Tigger's sandwiches.

"Are they stuck?" asked Piglet anxiously.

Pooh nodded.

"Couldn't you climb up to them?"

"I might, Piglet, and I might bring Roo down on my back, but I couldn't bring Tigger down. So we must think of something else." And in a thoughtful way he began to eat Roo's sandwiches, too.

Whether he would have thought of anything before he had finished the last sandwich, I don't know, but he had just got to the last one when there was crackling in the bracken, and Christopher Robin and Eeyore came strolling along together.

"I shouldn't be surprised if it hailed a good deal tomorrow," Eeyore was saying. "Blizzards and what-not. Being fine today doesn't Mean Anything. It has no sig—what's that word? Well, it has none of that. It's just a small piece of weather."

"There's Pooh!" said Christopher Robin, who didn't mind *what* it did tomorrow, as long as he was out in it. "Hallo, Pooh!"

"It's Christopher Robin!" said Piglet. "*He'll* know what to do."

They hurried up to him.

"Oh, Christopher Robin," began Pooh.

"And Eeyore," said Eeyore.

"Tigger and Roo are right up in the Six Pine Trees, and they can't get down, and—"

"And I was just saying," put in Piglet, "that if only Christopher Robin—"

"*And* Eeyore—"

"If only you were here, then we could think of something to do."

Christopher Robin looked up at Tigger and Roo, and tried to think of something.

"*I* thought," said Piglet earnestly, "that if Eeyore stood at the bottom of the tree, and if Pooh stood on Eeyore's back, and if I stood on Pooh's shoulders—"

"And if Eeyore's back snapped suddenly, then we could all laugh. Ha ha! Amusing in a quiet way," said Eeyore, "but not really helpful."

"Well," said Piglet meekly, "*I* thought—"

"Would it break your back, Eeyore?" asked Pooh, very much surprised.

"That's what would be so interesting, Pooh. Not being quite sure till afterwards."

Pooh said "Oh!" and they all began to think again.

"I've got an idea!" cried Christopher Robin suddenly.

"Listen to this, Piglet," said Eeyore, "and then you'll know what we're trying to do."

"I'll take off my tunic and we'll each hold a corner, and then Roo and Tigger can jump into it, and it will be all soft and bouncy for them, and they won't hurt themselves."

"*Getting Tigger down*," said Eeyore, "and *Not hurting anybody*. Keep those two ideas in your head, Piglet, and you'll be all right."

But Piglet wasn't listening, he was so agog at the thought of seeing Christopher Robin's blue braces again. He had only seen them once before, when he was much younger, and, being a little over-excited by them, had had to go to bed half an hour earlier than usual; and he had always wondered since if they were *really* as blue and as bracing as he had thought them. So when

Christopher Robin took his tunic off, and they were, he felt quite friendly to Eeyore again, and held the corner of the tunic next to him and smiled happily at him. And Eeyore whispered back: "I'm not saying there won't be an Accident *now*, mind you. They're funny things, Accidents. You never have them till you're having them."

When Roo understood what he had to do, he was wildly excited, and cried out: "Tigger, Tigger, we're going to jump! Look at me jumping, Tigger! Like flying, my jumping will be. Can Tiggers do it?" And he squeaked out: "I'm coming, Christopher Robin!" and he jumped—straight into the middle of the tunic. And he was going so fast that he bounced up again almost as high as where he was before—and went on bouncing and saying, "Oo!" for quite a long time—and then at last he stopped

and said, "Oo, lovely!" And they put him on the ground.

"Come on, Tigger," he called out. "It's easy."

But Tigger was holding on to the branch and saying to himself: "It's all very well for Jumping Animals like Kangas, but it's quite different for Swimming Animals like Tiggers." And he thought of himself floating on his back down a river, or striking out from one island to another, and he felt that that was really the life for a Tigger.

"Come along," called Christopher Robin. "You'll be all right."

"Just wait a moment," said Tigger nervously. "Small piece of bark in my eye." And he moved slowly along his branch.

"Come on, it's easy!" squeaked Roo. And suddenly Tigger found how easy it was.

"Ow!" he shouted as the tree flew past him.

"Look out!" cried Christopher Robin to the others.

There was a crash, and a tearing noise, and a confused heap of everybody on the ground.

Christopher Robin and Pooh and Piglet picked themselves up first, and then they picked Tigger up, and underneath everybody else was Eeyore.

"Oh, Eeyore!" cried Christopher Robin. "Are you hurt?" And he felt him rather anxiously, and dusted him and helped him to stand up again.

Eeyore said nothing for a long time. And then he said: "Is Tigger there?"

Tigger was there, feeling Bouncy again already.

"Yes," said Christopher Robin. "Tigger's here."

"Well, just thank him for me," said Eeyore.

Tigger Is Unbounced

One day Rabbit and Piglet were sitting outside Pooh's front door listening to Rabbit, and Pooh was sitting with them. It was a drowsy summer afternoon, and the Forest was full of gentle sounds, which all seemed to be saying to Pooh, "Don't listen to Rabbit, listen to me." So he got into a more comfortable position for not listening to Rabbit, and from time to time he opened his eyes to say "Ah!" and then closed them again to say "True," and from time to time Rabbit said, "You see what I mean, Piglet," very earnestly, and Piglet nodded earnestly to show that he did.

"In fact," said Rabbit, coming to the end of it at last, "Tigger's getting so Bouncy nowadays that it's time we taught him a lesson. Don't you think so, Piglet?"

Piglet said that Tigger *was* very Bouncy, and that if they could think of a way of unbouncing him, it would be a Very Good Idea.

"Just what I feel," said Rabbit. "What do *you* say, Pooh?"

Pooh opened his eyes with a jerk and said, "Extremely."

"Extremely what?" asked Rabbit.

"What you were saying," said Pooh. "Undoubtably."

Piglet gave Pooh a stiffening sort of nudge, and Pooh, who felt more and more that he was somewhere else, got up slowly and began to look for himself.

"But how shall we do it?" asked Piglet. "What sort of a lesson, Rabbit?"

"That's the point," said Rabbit.

The word "lesson" came back to Pooh as one he had heard before somewhere.

"There's a thing called Twy-stymes," he said. "Christopher Robin tried to teach it to me once, but it didn't."

"What didn't?" said Rabbit.

"Didn't what?" said Piglet.

Pooh shook his head.

"I don't know," he said. "It just didn't. What are we talking about?"

"Pooh," said Piglet reproachfully, "haven't you been listening to what Rabbit was saying?"

"I listened, but I had a small piece of fluff in my ear. Could you say it again, please, Rabbit?"

Rabbit never minded saying things again, so he asked where he should begin from; and when Pooh had said from the moment when the fluff got in his ear, and Rabbit had asked when that was, and Pooh had said he didn't know because he hadn't heard properly, Piglet settled it all by saying that what they were trying to do was, they were just trying to think of a way to get the bounces out of Tigger, because however much you liked him, you couldn't deny it, he *did* bounce.

"Oh, I see," said Pooh.

"There's too much of him," said Rabbit, "that's what it comes to."

Pooh tried to think, and all he could think of was something which didn't help at all. So he hummed it very quietly to himself.

If Rabbit
Was bigger
And fatter
And stronger,
Or bigger
Than Tigger,
If Tigger was smaller,
Then Tigger's bad habit
Of bouncing at Rabbit
Would matter
No longer,
If Rabbit
Was taller.

"What was Pooh saying?" asked Rabbit. "Any good?"

"No," said Pooh sadly. "No good."

"Well, I've got an idea," said Rabbit, "and here it is. We take Tigger for a long explore, somewhere where he's never been, and we lose him there, and next morning we find him again, and—mark my words—he'll be a different Tigger altogether."

"Why?" asked Pooh.

"Because he'll be a Humble Tigger. Because he'll be a Sad Tigger, a Melancholy Tigger, a Small and Sorry Tigger, and Oh-Rabbit-I-*am*-glad-to-see-you Tigger. That's why."

"Will he be glad to see me and Piglet, too?"

"Of course."

"That's good," said Pooh.

"I should hate him to go *on* being Sad," said Piglet doubtfully.

"Tiggers never go on being Sad," explained Rabbit. "They get over it with Astonishing Rapidity. I asked Owl, just to make sure, and he said that that's what they always get over it with. But if we can make Tigger feel Small and Sad just for five minutes, we shall have done a good deed."

"Would Christopher Robin think so?" asked Piglet.

"Yes," said Rabbit. "He'd say 'You've done a good deed, Piglet. I would have done it myself, only I happened to be doing something else. Thank you, Piglet.' And Pooh, of course."

Piglet felt very glad about this, and he saw at once that what they were going to do to Tigger was a good thing to do, and as Pooh and Rabbit were doing it with him, it was a thing which even a Very Small Animal could wake up in the morning and feel comfortable about doing. So the only question was, where should they lose Tigger?

"We'll take him to the North Pole," said Rabbit, "because it was a very long explore finding it, so it will be a very long explore for Tigger unfinding it again."

It was now Pooh's turn to feel very glad, because it was he who had first found the North Pole, and when they got there, Tigger would see a notice which said, "Discovered by Pooh, Pooh found it," and then Tigger would know, which perhaps he didn't know, the sort of Bear Pooh was. *That* sort of Bear.

So it was arranged that they should start next morning, and that Rabbit, who lived near Kanga and Roo and Tigger, should now go home and ask Tigger what he was doing tomorrow, because if he wasn't doing anything, what about coming for an explore and getting Pooh and Piglet to come too? And if Tigger said "Yes" that would be all right, and if he said "No"—

"He won't," said Rabbit. "Leave it to me." And he went off busily.

The next day was quite a different day. Instead of being hot and sunny, it was cold and misty. Pooh didn't mind for himself, but when he thought of all the honey the bees wouldn't be making, a cold and misty day always made him feel sorry for them. He said so to Piglet when Piglet came to fetch him, and Piglet said that he wasn't thinking of that so much, but of how cold

and miserable it would be being lost all day and night on the top of the Forest. But when he and Pooh had got to Rabbit's house, Rabbit said it was just the day for them, because Tigger always bounced on ahead of everybody, and as soon as he got out of sight, they would hurry away in the other direction, and he would never see them again.

"Not never?" asked Piglet.

"Well, not until we find him again, Piglet. Tomorrow, or whenever it is. Come on. He's waiting for us."

When they got to Kanga's house, they found that Roo was waiting too, being a great friend of Tigger's, which made it Awkward; but Rabbit whispered "Leave this to me" behind his paw to

Pooh, and went up to Kanga.

"I don't think Roo had better come," he said. "Not today."

"Why not?" said Roo, who wasn't supposed to be listening.

"Nasty cold day," said Rabbit, shaking his head. "And you were coughing this morning."

"How do you know?" asked Roo indignantly.

"Oh, Roo, you never told me," said Kanga reproachfully.

"It was a Biscuit Cough," said Roo, "not one you tell about."

"I think not today, dear. Another day."

"Tomorrow?" said Roo hopefully.

"We'll see," said Kanga.

"You're always seeing, and nothing ever happens," said Roo sadly.

"Nobody could see on a day like this, Roo," said Rabbit. "I don't expect we shall get very far, and then this afternoon we'll all—we'll all—we'll—ah, Tigger, there you are. Come on. Good-bye, Roo! This afternoon we'll—come on, Pooh! All ready? That's right. Come on."

So they went. At first Pooh and Rabbit and Piglet walked together, and Tigger ran around them in circles, and then, when the path got narrower, Rabbit, Piglet, and Pooh walked one after another, and Tigger ran round them in oblongs, and by-and-by, when the gorse got very prickly on each side of the path, Tigger ran up and down in front of them, and sometimes he bounced into Rabbit and sometimes he didn't. And as they got higher, the mist got thicker, so that Tigger kept disappearing, and then when you thought he wasn't there, there he was again, saying "I say, come on," and before you could say anything, there he wasn't.

Rabbit turned round and nudged Piglet.

"The next time," he said. "Tell Pooh."

"The next time," said Piglet to Pooh.

"The next what?" said Pooh to Piglet.

Tigger appeared suddenly, bounced into Rabbit, and disappeared again. "Now!" said Rabbit. He jumped into a hollow by the side of the path, and Pooh and Piglet jumped after him. They crouched in the bracken, listening. The Forest was very silent when you stopped and listened to it. They could see nothing and hear nothing.

"H'sh!" said Rabbit.

"I am," said Pooh.

There was a pattering noise…then silence again.

"Hallo!" said Tigger, and he sounded so close suddenly that Piglet would have jumped if Pooh hadn't accidentally been sitting on most of him.

"Where are you?" called Tigger.

Rabbit nudged Pooh, and Pooh looked about for Piglet to nudge, but couldn't find him, and Piglet went on breathing wet bracken as quietly as he could, and felt very brave and excited.

"That's funny," said Tigger.

There was a moment's silence, and then they heard him pattering off again. For a little longer they waited, until the Forest had become so still that it almost frightened them, and then Rabbit got up and stretched himself.

"Well?" he whispered proudly. "There we are! Just as I said."

"I've been thinking," said Pooh, "and I think—"

"No," said Rabbit. "Don't. Run. Come on."

And they all hurried off, Rabbit leading the way.

"Now," said Rabbit, after they had gone a little way, "we can talk. What were you going to say, Pooh?"

"Nothing much. Why are we going along here?"

"Because it's the way home."

"Oh!" said Pooh.

"I *think* it's more to the right," said Piglet nervously. "What do *you* think, Pooh?"

Pooh looked at his two paws. He knew that one of them was the right, and he knew that when you had decided which one of them was the right, then the other one was the left, but he never could remember how to begin.

"Well," he said slowly—

"Come on," said Rabbit. "I know it's this way."

They went on. Ten minutes later they stopped again.

"It's very silly," said Rabbit, "but just for the moment I—Ah, of course. Come on...."

"Here we are," said Rabbit ten minutes later. "No, we're not...."

"Now," said Rabbit ten minutes later, "I think we ought to be getting—or are we a little bit more to the right than I thought?..."

"It's a funny thing," said Rabbit ten minutes later, "how everything looks the same in a mist. Have you noticed it, Pooh?"

Pooh said that he had.

"Lucky we know the Forest so well, or we might get lost," said Rabbit half an hour later, and he gave the careless laugh which you give when you know the Forest so well that you can't get lost.

Piglet sidled up to Pooh from behind.

"Pooh!" he whispered.

"Yes, Piglet?"

"Nothing," said Piglet, taking Pooh's paw. "I just wanted to be sure of you."

When Tigger had finished waiting for the others to catch up, and they hadn't, and when he had got tired of having nobody to say, "I say, come on" to, he thought he would go home. So he trotted back; and the first thing Kanga said when she saw him was "There's a good Tigger. You're just in time for your Strengthening Medicine," and she poured it out for him. Roo said proudly, "I've *had* mine," and Tigger swallowed his and said, "So have I," and then he and Roo pushed each other about in a friendly way, and Tigger accidentally knocked over one or

two chairs by accident, and Roo accidentally knocked over one on purpose, and Kanga said, "Now then, run along."

"Where shall we run along to?" asked Roo.

"You can go and collect some fir-cones for me," said Kanga, giving them a basket.

So they went to the Six Pine Trees, and threw fir-cones at each other until they had forgotten what they came for, and they left the basket under the trees and went back to dinner. And it was just as they were finishing dinner that Christopher Robin put his head in the door.

"Where's Pooh?" he asked.

"Tigger dear, where's Pooh?" said Kanga. Tigger explained what had happened at the same time Roo was explaining about his Biscuit Cough and Kanga was telling them not both to talk at once, so it was some time before Christopher Robin guessed that Pooh and Piglet

and Rabbit were all lost in the mist on the top of the Forest.

"It's a funny thing about Tiggers," whispered Tigger to Roo, "how Tiggers *never* get lost."

"Why don't they, Tigger?"

"They just don't," explained Tigger. "That's how it is."

"Well," said Christopher Robin, "we shall have to go and find them, that's all. Come on, Tigger."

"I shall have to go and find them," explained Tigger to Roo.

"May I find them too?" asked Roo eagerly.

"I think not today, dear," said Kanga. "Another day."

"Well, if they're lost tomorrow, may I find them?"

"We'll see," said Kanga, and Roo, who knew what *that* meant, went into a corner, and practised jumping out at himself, partly because he wanted to practise this, and partly because he didn't want Christopher Robin and Tigger to think that he minded when they went off without him.

"The fact is," said Rabbit, "we've missed our way somehow."

They were having a rest in a small sand-pit on the top of the Forest. Pooh was getting rather tired of that sand-pit, and suspected it of following them about, because whichever direction they started in, they always ended up at it, and each time, as it came through the mist at them, Rabbit said triumphantly, "Now I know where we are!" and Pooh said sadly, "So do I," and Piglet said nothing. He had tried to think of something to say, but the only thing he could think of was, "Help, help!" and it seemed silly to say that, when he had Pooh and Rabbit with him.

"Well," said Rabbit, after a long silence in which nobody thanked him for the nice walk they were having, "we'd better get on, I suppose. Which way shall we try?"

"How would it be," said Pooh slowly, "if, as soon as we're out of sight of this Pit, we try to find it again?"

"What's the good of that?" said Rabbit.

"Well," said Pooh, "we keep looking for Home and not finding it, so I thought that if we looked for this Pit, we'd be sure not to find it, which would be a Good Thing, because then we might find something we *weren't* looking for, which might be just what we *were* looking for, really."

"I don't see much sense in that," said Rabbit.

"No," said Pooh humbly, "there isn't. But there was going to be when I began it. It's just that something happened to it on the way."

"If I walked away from this Pit, and then walked back to it, of *course* I should find it."

"Well, I thought perhaps you wouldn't," said Pooh. "I just thought."

"Try," said Piglet suddenly. "We'll wait here for you."

Rabbit gave a laugh to show how silly Piglet was, and walked into the mist. After he had gone a hundred yards, he turned and walked back again…and after Pooh and Piglet had waited twenty minutes for him, Pooh got up.

"I just thought," said Pooh. "Now then, Piglet, let's go home."

"But, Pooh," cried Piglet, all excited, "do you know the way?"

"No," said Pooh. "But there are twelve pots of honey in my cupboard, and they've been calling to me for hours. I couldn't hear them properly before, because Rabbit *would* talk, but if nobody says anything except those twelve pots, I *think,* Piglet, I shall know where they're calling from. Come on."

They walked off together; and for a long time Piglet said nothing, so as not to interrupt the pots; and then suddenly he made a squeaky noise…and an oo-noise…because now he began to know where he was; but he still didn't dare to say so out loud, in case he wasn't. And just when he was getting so sure of himself that it didn't matter whether the pots went on calling or not, there was a shout from in front of them, and out of the mist came Christopher Robin.

"Oh, there you are," said Christopher Robin carelessly, trying to pretend that he hadn't been Anxious.

"Here we are," said Pooh.

"Where's Rabbit?"

"I don't know," said Pooh.

"Oh—well, I expect Tigger will find him. He's sort of looking for you all."

"Well," said Pooh, "I've got to go home for something, and so has Piglet, because we haven't had it yet, and—"

"I'll come and watch you," said Christopher Robin.

So he went home with Pooh, and watched him for quite a long time…and all the time he was watching, Tigger was tearing round the Forest making loud yapping noises for Rabbit. And at last a very Small and Sorry Rabbit heard him. And the Small and Sorry Rabbit rushed through the mist at the noise, and it suddenly turned into Tigger; a Friendly Tigger, a Grand Tigger, a Large and Helpful Tigger, a Tigger who bounced, if he bounced at all, in just the beautiful way a Tigger ought to bounce.

"Oh, Tigger, I *am* glad to see you," cried Rabbit.